LEE

Too Into You

By

Jasmine Reneé

The characters and events portrayed in this book are fictitious. Any similarity to real persons, living or dead, is coincidental and not intended by the author.

ISBN-13: 979-8-218-65271-5

Cover design by: Jasmine Reneé Williamson with Canva
Printed in the United States of America

Dedication

I'll always cherish the time
It was real to me
Thank you
For what it's worth
I love you,
Unconditionally.

Contents

Author's Note

The stories section of the work is set up that the story of the relationship moves forward and the "encounters", we'll call them, occur in reverse. You can decide for yourself if it's what one might call a "happy ending". See what I did there?

Accompanying works round out the entirety. They are not in any particular order.

If you find yourself at the "destination" of life, you're probably dead. So take a breath and remember the gift of the journey, even when it sucks ass....not in the good way, if that's your thing.

Most importantly...and I can not stress this enough...

This is a work of entirely fiction. Any resemblance to actual persons, living or dead, is purely coincidental and unintentional.

Stories

What is stand your ground comedy?

If you're one of the lucky ones who's never needed to use a dating app, consider yourself fortunate. But for me, a 35 year old remote tech worker who loves being home, and goes to bed at a very reasonable hour—meeting someone in person presented its own challenges. I'd just been on a string of several not bad, but not great dates and found myself back on a dating app when I matched with Pete.

Pete was 40, European, fit and handsome. For our first date, we met up at a jazz bar in the West Village. Things were going well —good communication, fun dates and no pressure on being physical.

He was, however, a bike rider. If you're not familiar with NYC bike culture, it can be very intense. In a nutshell, if you are in the way (pedestrian or car) good luck. I didn't mind it per se, but it did pose logistical challenges for places to securely lock up the bike when spending time anywhere other than his apartment.

Things with Pete started getting dicey when he consistently started reschedule dates, and only called me "babe" when doing so. I knew I was out when we took a trip together and the most fun I had was when we were not together. It would be another month before I called it though. One day he text me and I just didn't care to respond. I meant to text him back. I did; but then a day turned into weeks and I just didn't feel like I could respond at that point. I apologized a few months later. He did not respond.

After a few dreams about sexual tension with an old friend, I thought perhaps my subconscious was telling me I was denying a part of myself. So I matched and went on a date with a woman, Denise. She was around my age, lived in New Jersey and did something fitness adjacent. Our date was in Hoboken, which took me an hour and a half to get to. Denise picked a waterfront restaurant, and drove.

I already knew I wasn't willing to make that trek on any kind of regular basis, since where she lived would take even longer to get to. In any case, the date was fine and she was lovely, but I quickly realized I was just missing hanging with my girlfriends.

Those were the more positive experiences. Other dates included the basic no-shows, generally boring/bad date and guys not taking the hint when I was clearly ready to call it a night. I was getting tired of constant notifications for matches, only to be disappointed by men who had clearly not actually read my profile re: what I was looking for and interested in. So I took charge and turned off the notifications, but I kept swiping and expanded the age range that I'd be willing to entertain.

Then, one day, someone genuinely interesting showed up on my screen. In his first picture, he was in a nice suit and his chin length hair was slightly swooped over his face. It caught my eye enough to keep scrolling, but I didn't have great hope he was real. As I scrolled and read through the rest of the profile, my curiosity only increased.

Lee was 54, had an older daughter, lived in Manhattan, and seemed to have a full life of adventure. His bio suggested he was interested in culture, bettering himself and acting intentionally. If he was real, he was someone I wanted to know. Plus, he was incredibly handsome with a side of mischevious charm.

So, I swiped right, hoping for the best, but not expecting much. It was a match. Rather pleased, but still skeptical, I sent a message.

At least he'd know that I was real and had read his profile.

"You built a house from the ground up?" I asked.

With notifications turned off, it was two days later when I remembered I'd sent the message and checked the app. I was delighted to see he'd replied.

"It was my (now ex) wife's dream and I thought I could make it happen. How's your week been?"

A direct answer to my question and a relevant question in return —so far so good, maybe Lee wasn't a bot afterall. It would be slow going in terms of frequency, but we exchanged messages every couple of days for the next couple of weeks. We landed on hobbies, and he asked what I was into.

"Admittedly, I'm a bit of a home body, but I love jazz and live theatre. I'm also really into stand-up comedy."

His response was unexpectedly "what is stand your ground comedy?"

I started to panic, just a little. I had no idea what that was, or could be, and was worried I needed to unmatch him immediately. Fortunately, upon scrolling up to my message, I realized that "stand up" had been auto corrected to "stand your ground." I promptly cleared that up.

The typo must have convinced him I was real, and Lee asked if we should meet up and grab a drink. We exchanged numbers and set a date for the coming week. The best part? Neither one of us had to take a train or leave the borough. Hell, neither one of us had to leave the neighborhood and that was already a win in my book.

I had no idea what to expect, or if I was even ok with dating a man 19 years older than me. There was just something about our conversation that made me want to know more about him and his experiences. Even if there was no chemistry, I was sure I'd at least learn something new.

Will you fuck me goodbye?

My heart is broken and currently racing as I stand in front of Lee's apartment door, and not from the five flights of stairs I've just climbed. I am here to make my case, in person. I am here to ask Lee to fuck me one last time.

I remove my coat and put it in my bag, praying the neighbor doesn't open their door and see me in nothing but heels. I take a deep breath, smile, put my left hand on my hip and knock on the door with my right. A few seconds later, which feels like forever, Lee opens the door. His eyes widen as he takes in the view.

"Wow. Umm...what are you doing here?" inquiring, seemingly trying to focus on my face, but failing to maintain eye contact.

"I need a favor. If you'll oblige, I want you to fuck me one last time." I pause a moment and remind myself to ask for what I want. "Will you fuck me goodbye?"

The silence is palpable, and I lose all sense of time. Now, Lee is looking into my eyes. My eyes return the gaze, pleading. No matter how many times I've played this scenario in my head, I'm simply not prepared for him to reject me-- again. He doesn't say a word, but steps aside and gestures his arm into the apartment.

Normally, I'd confidently make my way in but this is new territory and I still don't have an answer. He is inviting me in though, so signs point to a potential yes. I pick up my bag and walk just past him into the entryway. Without a word, he closes the door and turns to face me. He looks me up and down and, what I'm hoping is a playful smirk, begins to form on the right side of his mouth. He reaches for my bag and I hand it to him with a tight lipped smile.

He hangs the bag on the key hook and moves towards me. He places his hands on my hips and pushes his body into mine. My back is against the wall and the gap between us no longer exists. Now I'm certain it's a smirk.

He leans in and kisses me. It's familiar, wanting, and perfect. I wrap my arms around his neck and run my fingers through his hair. I pull his lips away from mine. I want an answer.

"So is that a yes?"

"Yes, please."

I let out a small laugh as I recall the many times I'd said that to him. I feel the tension leave my body and notice the heightened sensations of Lee's clothed skin against my naked body.

This was not a rejection mission. The comfort of familiarity takes hold and I lead him towards the living room. Not much has changed in the space and I take calming breaths as memories begin to flood my mind. Fortunately, it's a short walk to the blue chair and I direct him to sit down.

"You, sir, have on too much clothing."

I straddle him in the chair, removing his shirt clumsily as he captures my nipple in his mouth. I watch as he licks, sucks and kisses both nipples; then I begin removing his pants and underwear. For this, I receive no interference.

"Mmm, much better." I return my lips to his, holding his face in my hands as he slides his hands up my back.

"Indeed. What do we do now?"

I laugh. "Well, what do you want to do?"

"I want to eat you."

His cock twitches when he says it, and now I'm the one with a smirk. He's made this request before, but this time feels almost naughty. I welcome his desire, but decide to tease him first.

I stand, turn away from him and fold in half so he has an unfettered view and full access to my pussy and ass. One hand braced on the floor, I take the other and run my fingers across my very wet labia and down to my clit. My body contracts to my own touch.

Lee slides foward to the edge of the chair. "Fuck, that's hot." I smile and watch through my legs as he takes my hand from my clit and sucks my fingers. Then he grabs both sides of my hips and plants his tongue in my slit—in and out and up and down—flicking and swirling the tip around my clit when it's near. His lips meet my lower lips and an appreciative moan escapes from us both.

I reluctantly pull away from him and stand. Turning to face him, I lower myself to my knees, stopping for a kiss.

"I love the taste of me on you."

"I love the taste of you on me."

I quickly use the tie on my wrist to put my hair in a messy bun. His cock rests on his leg, semi hard and waiting to reach it's full potential.

"I've thought about this a lot." Lee says—his eyes giving away the truth of the statement. It's all the encouragement I need.

My hand strokes while my mouth sucks. Occasionally I remove my hand and take him to the back of my throat. I know this won't last long—not because Lee doesn't enjoy it, but because he wants to be inside me, in the moist pink cavern between my legs.

"Let's go to the bedroom. I want to feel you quiver."

He stands and grabs my hand to lead me. I'd normally protest and suggest moving to the couch—a dance we'd also done many times before, but I want to feel him inside me and fuck me just as much as he wants to be there and do it.

I grab my vibrator from my bag on the way to the bedroom. Lee bends me over the side of the bed as I place the vibrator on my clit. He rubs the head of his penis through the moisture of my vagina, teasing. As the first wave of my orgasm arrives, he thrusts himself fully inside me.

I really like you

We were several dates in and having a fun time. I'd never found myself so genuinely interested in knowing more about someone. Lee was full of stories and was quite captivating, but this particular date showed he could be gracious and roll with the punches.

It was my turn to pick our date activity. You know, when the relationship is still new and you're trying to do fun things and come up with original date ideas. I had picked a cooking class. I was expecting a kitchen stet up with stations and fresh, customizeable ingredients to cater to each of our dietary restrictions. Unfortunately, what we got was preparation at tables in a hotel bar, premixed dumpling stuffing and a couple minutes of sautéing and pan frying on a camp style gas burner.

We spend the time laughing, chatting and listening; both of us taking it in stride and eventually agreeing to leave early and go have a proper dinner back uptown in our neighborhood. We decided on a cute Italian spot and sat at the bar.

"Ok, surely you have questions. Let's hear 'em."

I was diving in. I'd asked on a previous date if there was anything in particular he wanted to know about me. He admitted there was and that he'd think about it and let me know.

His first question certainly did not disappoint.

"Have you dated older men before?" then continued "Is that something you 'do'?"

I could have been appalled, but I was actually rather amused. It was a valid question, but I had my own money and truthfully never saw myself with anyone "much" older than me.

"I usually date men that are older than me, but not by this much. I'd say low to mid 40s is the highest. Though I did go on three dates with someone that was 55. But no, it's not something I 'do'. And what about you?"

"No, I don't really date younger women. Most of my past relationships have actually been with women older than me."

The next few questions were much less exciting—ranging from tattoos to favorite colors—six and zero and pink and blue for myself and him, respectively.

"Have you been back on the app? How's dating going? Are you seeing anyone else?"

Lee's questions were forward, intentional and direct-- unnerving but mostly appreciated.

"Honestly, I've not really been back on the app. I'm looking to share my life with someone, but I'm not in a rush and I'm a bit busy so I haven't really had too much time. Our dates are usually on my available evenings anyway. But no, I'm not seeing anyone else."

He nodded. I waitied a few seconds to allow him time to offer more, but he didn't. So I again, turned the question back to him.

"Why do you ask? Have you been on?"

"No, I haven't been back on the app. I'm not really interested in anything else at the moment."

The smile forming on my face was difficult to keep hidden as I playfully retorted.

"Oh yeah? Why's that?"

You know that moment in the movie where the guy says the perfect thing and you're like that would never happen in real life? Well, this was that moment.

"Because I really like you and I'm hoping you like me too."

He looked at me as he said it, then turned and took a sip of his drink, as though he'd said something he shouldn't.

I nodded my head, thinking, processing—trying to figure out what to say or how to respond. The truth is, I had told my therapist just a couple days before that I was beginning to like him. I also hadn't quite reconciled with myself if 19 years was an acceptable age difference. I've never been one to shy away from an experience or new opportunity without some thought or the 'ol college try. Dating Lee had been no exception, but I wasn't leaping to any conclusions.

This evening had been different though. I wasn't embarrassed that the activity portion of the date had been a flop. I had had so much fun just being with him and talking to him. I wanted to know more about this man and I didn't want there to be any question regarding my interest in continuing to see him. I opened my mouth and spoke honestly.

"I really like you too."

Now were were both smiling. He leaned in to kiss me and I didn't move away. It was soft and quick, but so lovely. It was getting late and he had a flight to cath the next day. We paid the check and started walking towards our respective apartments.

Lee grabbed my hand and didn't let go till we arrived at our usual goodbye corner. He only let go of my hand to bring my face to his to kiss me more. As my hands began to slide up the back of his neck and grip on to his hair, I remembered we were on a street corner, in front of a closed store, making out like teenagers, and pulled away.

"I'm not a 'make out on the corner' kind of gal." He laughed and agreed with the sentiment. "Safe travels tomorrow and keep me posted."

He kissed me once more, lingering, hovering his lips over mine.

"I will. Have a good night."

It had finally happened, the good night kiss..well, any kiss. He had taken the initiative and I was grateful. It was important to me that I didn't force the physical. I was doing things differently with Lee. While the kiss was admittedly worth the wait, it had been over a month and several dates coming. I hoped he wouldn't stop kissing me. As turned on as I was, after that kiss, I had a feeling I'd want more than a make out on a street corner next time.

Lee left for the weekend to see an old friend and meet his new fiancé. He text me every morning and called me a couple of times. He sent me pictures from his run and lunch on the bay in San Diego. I never asked Lee if he'd told his friend about me, but I didn't feel the need. We were communicating despite the distance and time difference. Though I was ready for his return and our next make out—or perhaps a little more.

Magnificent cock

"Let's go up to the roof."

Lee knows what I want, but the hesitation in his movement and raised eyebrow suggests I might not get it tonight, if ever. I bite my lip and smile mischievously reaching my hand for his. Still nothing, so I pout and ask "please?" His expression softens and he takes my outstretched hand as I lead us out of the apartment and up the stairs. Being on the top floor of the walk up has its advantages, including a short walk to the roof and almost exclusive use of it.

Its around 8:30pm and 77 degrees with a slight breeze, quite comfortable and most importantly, dark. The door to the roof only locks from the inside with a latch hook, so I lean against it and place my hands over my head, grabbing an elbow with each hand, relinquishig control. I look at Lee and raise my left eyebrow as if to ask what he is waiting for.

Taking the hint, he approaches to kiss me. I wrap my hands around the back of his neck, pulling him closer as passion builds. He pulls at the tie on my robe opening it to reveal my body, hard nipples included. I moan quietly, in approval, as he moves his hands around my torso downward until he grabs my ass, squeezing hard and pressing himself against me.

He slides his mouth from my lips, across my chin. He makes his way to my ear, my neck, my shoulder until he's at my nipple. He kisses it lightly, swirls his tongue around it, then puts it in his mouth and sucks. Before I'm ready, he releases my nipple and continues his downward trail of kisses.

Lee kneels. I watch him see his the glimmer of my hood piercing and smile. His eyes move upwards towards mine as he kisses my thigh. Our eyes meet and we wait. Its a short game to see who will give in to their desires first.

"Turn around. I want to eat you from behind."

I guess it's him, but I have a strong feeling we'll both come out as winners.

I turn, facing the door, still leaning against it to prevent interruption, or at least buy some time. He flips the bottom of the robe onto my back, then puts his palms on my ass and slides his tongue up my inner thigh until it reaches my clit. Reminding myself we are very much not in the confines of a sound proofed bedroom, I mumble a muffled "Fuck, yes baby" through the hand and robe material with which I'm covering my mouth.

"Yes, yes, yes." His tongue muscle is skillful, alternating licking, flicking and circles. He removes a hand from my ass, and then I feel his fingers inside me. The air catches in my throat as I inhale sharply, but I settle into the stimulation begins to slowly finger fuck me.

Lee repositions himself against the door, now facing my lady bits, and continues pleasuring me. I close my eyes and imagine he's stroking his cock. My body responds to the pleasure and the visual. I find myself again moaning into terry cloth.

"I want to feel you inside me" I say as I reluctantly pull his mouth away from my throbbing pussy.

Lee stands and I kiss him, savoring myself on his lips and tongue. I tug at the tie on his robe. As it opens and I place my index finger on the tip of his cock, pleasantly met with precum. I bring my finger to my mouth to taste it.

“This is so fucking hot....” escapes from his lips in a whisper. I kneel and allow his cock entry to the back of my throat. I alternate stroking, sucking and deep throating. I place his hands on the sides of my head and move his hips back and forth till we have a rhythm.

“This feels incredible, but I want to fuck your pussy and feel you squeeze around me.”

I slide my mouth off his cock— “Mmm.”

“Yeah, but let’s go to the bedroom.”

Lee helps me stand, and pulls me into him, our bodies firmly against the door. I think he is about to kiss me, but grabs my nipples,and squeezes. Hard. Just like I like it.

“Fuck." I mew. "Okay, okay inside. You keep that up and I won’t be able to be quiet.”

“That might have been the idea.”

“You’ve gotten me quite wet.”

“Let's see.”

Lee turns me around by my hips so my back is to his chest. I instinctively bend over. He grabs his cock and slides it up and down the entrance of my vagina, pausing just at the entrance.

“You’re such a tease, Lee. Just fuck me.”

Technically a request, but also a desirous command. I don’t think he’ll mind me being direct. I am correct. He thrusts his cock in my pussy and slowly removes it several times, continuing to tease. Unfortunately, its getting more difficult to both be quiet and hold myself steady.

Lee pulls out once more, helps me stand, and rushes us back inside, down the stairs and into his bedroom. He likes me laying over the side of the bed, once again, on full display. I'm happy to oblige and place the nearby vibrator on my clit as a visual invitation to pick up where we'd left off on the roof.

A short while of faster, slower, and deeper strokes, our orgasms arrive. I make a mental note of his magnificent his cock is.

I want to eat you

“What am I missing?” I asked Lee, looking up at him, my head resting on his chest.

“What do you mean?”

“I don’t know...like what’s wrong with you? Are you wanted? Do you owe the IRS a shit ton of money? Are you dying? Are you married?” I just blurted out whatever popped into my mind.

Lee was amused, chuckling as he answered. “Not wanted. Have some debt, but not a lot. Do not owe the IRS that I know of. In pretty good shape and I have divorce papers that definitively declare that I am no longer married.”

“Is there anyone under the impression that they are in a relationship with you?”

His brow furrowed as he considered and deciphered what I as asking. “Not that I’m aware of. I am single.”

Inwardly, I breathed a sigh of relief. Outwardly, I nuzzled deeper into his chest. We were not yet having penetrative sex. Not for lack of desire on my part. I had worn lingerie in his favorite color, pastel blue, and made no secret of my wish for him to see the ensemble during our dinner conversation. Walking towards his apartment from the train he’d said “I’d like to eat you, but I don’t want to have sex yet.” Seemed like a reasonable compromise to me.

So here we were, cuddling naked and I was asking questions I probably should have asked at dinner, or anytime prior to having sat on his face. Nevertheless, the conversation was easy and comfortable and I was enjoying the closeness. It was getting late though and we both had early mornings.

After a few good night kisses and some lingering at the door, I was making my way down five flights, across six blocks and up two flights to my apartment. I smiled the whole way home; probably looking like a crazy person. I didn't care. This was something different, something wonderful and something that felt real. I was ready to let this turn into whatever it was going to become.

Things seemed to be getting more serious. The dates were more frequent. Lee had invited me to his meditation class and introduced me as his girlfriend. I had finally overcome my superstition that if I started telling my friends about him that something would go wrong. Our bodies stayed in close proximity, we had deep chats about life, health and creativity; and we were easily having some of the best sex I'd ever had.

Lee's "I really like you" had garnered a few more "reallys" and I started expanding my circle of who knew about him. We were trying to move slowly, trying to be careful and not get in over our heads, but the feelings were there and they were strong. It felt like when he held my hand, it wasn't out of obligation, but because his hand felt empty without mine in it.

Lee and I both valued mental health and would often share what we were learning or had discovered in our therapy sessions. I'd never been so open, honest and vulnerable with a partner and it felt amazing. Lee was relatively new to his journey and he was honest about not being sure how he felt about the things he was learning about himself. It was clear to me that I was falling in love; and I knew he'd be the great love of my life or he'd break my fucking heart.

The next month was going to be busy and we wouldn't see each other much, as Lee was headed to his daughter's graduation for a long weekend and I was headed to Australia for a couple weeks. I stopped by his place the night before he left. He was feeling frustrated about being in close quarters with his ex-wife, his daughter's mother.

"When you find yourself getting frustrated, just remember that your baby girl is graduating. And remember how proud you are of her and that you're there to celebrate her."

"Thank you. I'll try to remember that."

It was a quick stop. I kissed him goodbye and wished him safe travels.

The next morning, Lee left and I barely heard from him over the next few days. It was a stark difference from his trip to see his best friend. I'd normally wake up to a voice note with a good morning and well wishes for the day, but I got zero voice notes. I did get a text with a picture post ceremony.

My texts remained largely unresponded. I was being "left on read." I tried not to let my thoughts get the best of me. I knew his daughter and his ex had no clue I even existed. I wasn't trying to rush Lee into sharing anything he wasn't ready to share yet, but part of me couldn't help but think he was hiding me too. That was my own issue to deal with though, and I needed to ask if I wanted the answers.

Lee called when he got to the airport on his way back to NY, as if it wasn't the first time I'd heard his voice in several days. I was happy to hear from him anyway and we set a time to meet in a couple of days. The morning voice notes and regular texting intervals returned.

"Things felt different when you were gone." I told him when we got together. "I have been a secret and hidden in a relationship before and I didn't care for it. I don't need you to tell everyone about me, but your communication could have been better. And I know you were spending time with your daughter and it was busy, but it just felt different."

I never thought I'd have the confidence to share these feelings with a partner for fear of sounding like a whiny little bitch, but Lee didn't make me feel bad about it.

"You're right. I could have been more communicative. I'm not trying to make excuses, but it just felt non stop and like I didn't have time. I was sleeping on the couch and the second I went to bed it felt like it was time to wake up, and I didn't have much privacy either and didn't want to disturb anyone."

"I'm not blaming you, Lee. You didn't do anything wrong, and you're not in trouble. I'm just sharing how I felt."

Our sushi order was delivered and we had dinner sitting cross legged on either side of his coffee table. It was easily one of the most romantic dinner dates we'd had. I just kept stealing glances at him and smiling, thinking how lucky I was to have this man in my life who I didn't want to hide from. Who showed me, mostly, that he cared about me and valued openness and honestly.

I so wanted to tell him I loved him, but I couldn't bring myself to say the words. I didn't think he was ready to hear it. Or I was just afraid to say it because I didn't know what would happen. It's not like the subject of love hadn't come up, it had; but I was already out on a limb being transparent about my feelings. Besides, he'd started it with his "I really like you." Come to think of it, I hadn't heard that in a while either.

A few days later, Lee helped me load my suitcase in to the car as I left to head to the airport. I didn't want to go. I'd booked this trip the year before we'd even met. My travel had slowed significantly, as I was focused on building a life I didn't feel the need to escape from. It felt like if I went on this trip, the life I'd been working to build would try to escape from me. Nevertheless, I kissed Lee goodbye and got in the car to head off to the land down under for two weeks.

I love you

Lee stares deeply into my eyes with the warmest, boyish and most charming smile.

"I love you."

I smile back at him and stand on my tip toes to meet his lips for a kiss. I'd been waiting months to hear him say those words. His actions had been showing it for weeks, but here was the audio confirmation.

I feel like I'm floating as he slides his hands down my body, landing on the small of my back, but not before he reaches down to squeeze my ass. I offer a half moan, half chuckle through our lips and run my fingers through his hair. It's a passionate and heated kiss, as if our tongues are fencing.

Lee pulls my dress over my head and I remove his shirt. He lowers himself to his knees in front of me and slides my underwear down. Peeking up at me, he raises his eyebrows twice. I wait, expectantly, for him to slide his tongue over my clit. Ever the tease, he starts kissing my inner thighs, up to my hip bones and across to my happy trail.

My heart is beating faster and I'm struggling to maintain focus on my own sensations. My eyes are closed and I can feel the coolness of his breath in contrast to the warmth of my body. My breaths are sporatic.

I remain still in anticipation, ready for the next wave of sensation—a flick of his tongue, his fingers sliding in, a nipple squeeze—but I feel nothing.

My eyes open and I'm in my bedroom, alone. It was just another morning. Lee hadn't told me he loved me. We were not about to have amazing sex. It was just a dream.

My boyfriend thinks so too

The two weeks in Australia were full of adventure. I went on a hot air balloon ride, skydived on to a beach and saw a sea turtle while snorkeling at the Great Barrier Reef... what's left of it anyway.

My relationship was also on it's own journey. In spite of the 16 hour time difference, we exchanged voice messages at generally appropriate times, but things were different. "Good morning, beautiful" was replaced with "Hey there". You know how you can hear stress and disractedness in someone's tone? Listening to his messages felt like someone trying to engage who has already checked out.

Don't get me wrong. Lee was in the middle of two big roll outs at work, that were not going well, and he was stressed. He made time to send me a voice message during the day just before I was off to bed. So the distraction makes sense too, but there was more.

It's difficult to explain, but it felt like he was going through the motions. There was no real connection behind the words except when he was encouraging me to go do something, and not be communicating with him.

One such activity was to meet up with a guy I had met in Thailand, that happened to live in Melbourne. I hesitated to meet up with this guy because I was pretty sure he was interested in me. After a long day, an upcoming early morning flight and jetlag, I'd sent the guy an apologetic message.

"Hey! I'm exhausted and I won't be able to meet up later. Let me know if you ever come to New York though!"

“That’s a bummer as I thought you were quite cute.”

“Thank you. My boyfriend thinks so too.”

I never told Lee about that interaction. I started to; took a screenshot and everything, but I never sent it. I guess I didn’t want him to be concerned because I was not interested in that guy. I think I was also afraid Lee might not discourage me from seeing what happened.

Lee's voice memos got shorter and he’d make comments that he didn’t think his would be as long as mine. It sounded like obligation city, population 1. My notes wer(e longer because I had lots to share from each day. I’d send a voice note and a few pictures of the highlights of my day.

Come to think of it, he didn't send me any pictures while I was away. He wasn't on an Australian adventure, but it would have been nice to see what he was having for dinner (probably sushi) or a link to what he was listening to that evening on Spotify. I wanted to be in the loop, hear about his day, share his life—even from several thousands of miles away. I didn't need his voice notes to be long. I just wanted them to be real and honest.

I couldn’t sleep one evening, well early morning, around 3am Australia time. I figured he’d be home resting and enjoying the evening, so I text him. We caught up for a bit over text. I so wanted to actually talk to him, hear his voice in real time, but he basically ushered me off to sleep. It didn’t feel great.

The trip was coming to a close though, and I hoped we could figure things out—that they’d get back to “normal” when I returned. I sent my last voice note just before my flight took off from Sydney, to arrive in NY on Saturday morning.

"I'm so excited to be coming home. I miss the kitties and my bed and you. I don't want to make assumptions, but I'm hoping we can hang out tomorrow. I know you have meditation in the morning and will want to write in the afternoon, but maybe the evening?"

Lee text back "Yeah. I'll let you know, but that should work."

At no point did I think Lee was cheating on me. Idiotic? Maybe. His relationship past wasn't exactly squeaky clean and mine had it's own detours. But he hadn't given me a reason to think he was being unfaithful. And frankly, if he was going to cheat, there wasn't a fucking thing I could do about it.

I didn't share what time my plane was landing. If I made it back early enough, I was gonna go home, drop off my bags, say hello to the kitties and head to his place for a kiss before he started his Saturday routine. It all worked out and I stood outside his apartment, waiting and excited to see him.

Lee came down with headphone in his ears, recycling boxes in his hands and a preoccupied look on his face. When he saw me, it took a few seconds to register in his mind. Not exactly the hello I was hoping for or how I thought it would go, but I was looking at his actual face and ready to figure out what was going on with us.

"Hey..." Lee is hesitant and a little confused. I approach him slowly with a smile as he continues "Hey. I didn't know you were gonna be back so early, now I feel bad." He breaks down the boxes and shoves them in the bins.

"No, no. Don't feel bad. I knew you had class and would probably write later too. I have errands to run and I scheduled some furniture delivery to keep me busy and awake." All of which I said honestly.

"Have you been out here long?"

"No." That was a half lie. "Just a few minutes. I very selfishly just wanted to kiss you. I missed you."

Finished with the boxes, Lee finally fully acknowledges me--with a side hug and a peck on the lips. It was not the "I'm so glad to see you. I missed you too. Can't wait to fuck you later" kiss I thought it might be, but his lips were on mine.

The kiss end too soon.

"I feel bad, but I need to go. I was just on a call about work stuff and am running behind this morning."

I give him my biggest smile. "It's okay, babe. Go. Text me later." Lee gives me another quick kiss and heads off towards the train.

Jet lag kicks my ass all day. At one point I give in and take a nap, but only for 25 minutes. It's a technique Lee told me about that he learned from a Norwegian boat captain. It worked wonders. Though I had been at Lee's around 7:50am, I didn't hear from him until 5pm. I had thought it would have been closer to 2pm.

We agreed to meet at his place and see where the evening took us. The only place I wanted to be was in his arms. He mentioned he hadn't eaten and I hadn't either. He said he'd make us a snack, then we could go have dinner.

The five-flight stair climb was as annoying as ever, but my mind was preoccupied with what I hoped would be welcome back sex, and a much better hello than this morning. Lee was at the door, waiting for me, with that boyish smirk I loved. He welcomed me into his apartment and kissed me like he missed me. There it was. That familiar, desirous,wanting physicality that was intoxicatingly sexy.

"Should we go to the bedroom first and snack after?"

I was hoping he'd ask that. Now we were on the same page.

"Mmm, you read my mind. Let's."

For the next few hours, our bodies were back in sync. We had a lovely evening catching up. I so enjoyed being around Lee. I really had missed him. Something was still off though. I couldn't put my finger on it. I wanted him to just tell me, talk to me, share with me, and fill me in. I didn't have to wait long.

Sex on the couch

I'm listening to Lee share what he learned in therapy and was struggling with. He'd cancelled our date the evening before because of it. I love that he feels comfortable to share it with me. I'm not his therapist, but I want him to know that he can always share, and I'll always listen--no judgement.

I straddle his lap and hug him tight, then sit back and look into his eyes.

"I may not know the words to say or be able to help, but I'll always listen and just be here for you."

"Thank you."

"And I so appreciate your sharing with me, Lee. But know that you don't have to just because you feel you should. I want you to share because you want to."

"I know. I do want to." I actually think he means it.

I kiss him softly. One kiss turns into two, then three, the intensity builds, and before long we're making out on the couch. Lee pulls me in closer, impressing his desire upon me. I support myself with one hand the couch behind him. The other slides up his chest, up the side of his neck to the back of his head, until my fingers are in his hair. I love running my fingers through his soft, only slightly grey tresses, pausing for light grabs and tugs as I move through. I can feel myself getting wet.

As if he can feel it to, Lee voices his desire to be inside me.

There's no better way to find yourself inside of a woman than asking her, making your desire known. The "yes" that follows, should it, is that of a woman who is geared up and ready for her pleasure and yours.

Lee removes my pants and I lift my hips to assist. I allow a few extra seconds for him to remove his pants as I brace on the armrest behind him.

He's hard. I'm wet. We're both ready. I lower back into his lap, guiding his cock inside me. We probably look like teenagers trying to fuck in a hurry. Our shirts are still on, his pants are around his ankles and the position isn't doing either of us any favors. It doesn't matter though. This is the kind of quick and dirty sex that functions as an exchange.

The exchange of power, of trust, of vulnerability. He wants to fuck me to reclaim his sense of strength, to prove he's not soft or weak. He feels he's said too much and doesn't know how to take it back or what I might think of him as a man. He's scared and he's grasping at a way to close the door to the piece of himself that's exposed.

Sex is safe. I give myself freely, willing my body to show Lee that I don't doubt his strength. He is the same man I fell in love with and there's no need to close the door. I just want us to love and support one another. I squeeze myself around him--physically and metaphorically.

I ride him. He fucks me. We find a rhythm together. Grinding against and bouncing on his dick are easily two of my top five greatest pleasures. The sex lasts only a few minutes and we don't change positions. Lee grabs my hips and manages a few more thrusts before his return to confidence is complete. The sounds of his orgasm and the subsequent warmth of his cum inside me take another two spots on the list. The final cuddling spot does not happen this time.

I can't do this

It was Wednesday night—date night--a few days after my return from Australia. We'd hung out on Saturday and he'd come by for a quick fuck on Sunday, but tonight was our designated time to hang. The first night in the week that we were available to see one another.

I looked forward to it, even though it was also Lee's therapy day. I never quite knew how he'd be feeling or what he'd say. I was never afraid or terribly worried, but I did consider that the things he was discovering and discussing could have an impact on the relationship.

Lee's actions still reflected that he cared for me. He still made the effort to see me. Sure, the communication that had been a bit off while I was away, but here we were having date night, cooking in his kitchen.

"I worry that my feelings for you aren't as consistent as your feelings for me. It's not you, though. It's how I feel about me. I feel like I could wake up one day and realize I can't do this anymore."

I just nodded, staring into my wine glass. He looked at me for a bit, trying to gauge my reaction, then followed up.

"Do you have any thoughts on that? Does that scare you?"

"Lee, my feelings for you do not waiver. I have no idea why, but that doesn't scare me. I mean, that's how relationships work, right? At any point, either one of us could decide we don't want to do this anymore."

My mind flashed back to an earlier relationship moment when we were laying in bed. Lee was looking down at me as I laid across his lap, tracing my body with his hands. He wasn't there mentally, his eyes were unfocused. I asked him where he went and he mumbled something along the lines of "just thinking". In that moment, I knew he would be the great love of my life, or he would break my fucking heart.

I returned to the present moment, knowing the heart break part was coming as he finished cooking. Dinner was ready and Lee asked how much I wanted. I told him I wasn't very hungry. I was silent for the next hour.

He made himself a plate and sat on the couch. I joined him with my newly refreshed glass of wine. We listened to the jazz playlist he'd turned on—my favorite. He usually opted for EDM. The jazz was the perfect planned chaos to the seemingly nonsensical peace in my head.

I stood up from the couch and held out my hand to him. He grabbed it and joined me. We stood in the center of the living room and I wrapped my arms around him, swaying to the music. I nuzzled my head against his chest and took a deep breath.

"That makes me feel like a sitting duck." I pause to consider how to continue. My thoughts are still not composed, even in the calm. "I deserve to be with someone who knows how they feel about me and knows they want to be with me. Relationships take work and I've been in this one on your terms. That's not on you at all, it's on me. I've allowed it."

I looked up at Lee. It was my turn to try to gauge a response. He looked back at me and I didn't see anything, let alone answers. I hadn't actually asked for any. Lee moves to kiss me and I let him. His kiss feels warm, his arms are strong and firm around me. The thoughts of break up and loss and sadness begin to melt away.

"Can we just do what we're good at?"

Lee's question took the final wind out of my sails. Of course I was pleased to hear he also enjoyed our sex life. I wanted nothing more than to allow his physical penetration to plug the methaphorical hole that had started forming in the space that he'd filled in my heart.

What my mind translated his question to was "I don't want to deal with this just let me have the part of you I want right now. Let's take the easy way out of this tonight."

The truth is, my heart already knew, so my subconcious started to process the end. I didn't know how long I had until it was officially over, but right then, he still wanted to be mine and I wanted to be his one last time.

I said the only thing that came to mind. "Yes, please."

The first time

On the couch, with Lee in front of me, I watch him spread me open with his fingers. As the pink reveals itself, I sense him get lost in it. He moves in closer to taste me.

I'd generally close my eyes and enjoy the sensations, but I want to watch him. I want to try something different with him and discover what I might be missing when my eyes are closed.

Lee doesn't notice. He's mesmerized by the colors, taste and smell of my pussy. I don't spend much time looking at it, but I have come to appreciate it, in its own way, over the years.

He gently slides his fingers around the entrance of my vagina. We've talked about my not being a fan of fingers, especially if there's no moisture to support a smooth insertion. I'm certain I'm quite wet and that would not be a problem right now, but he opts to use his tongue, gliding all the way up to my clit. He starts sucking, then I feel his fingers slide into me.

I rather enjoy the view of his face burried between my legs. I think about asking him to look at me, but don't want to interrupt the focus on his lingual and phalangeal efforts. So I continue to observe and note how my body responds.

Lee removes his fingers and starts strokes his cock. I've not seen him do this before; and fuck is the idea of him using me as lube sexy. My inner monologue of dirty talk begins. Outwardly, I moan and my uterus begins its wave of contractions. Lee looks up at me with a pleased grin. I give in, my eyes closing and enjoy.

It's a quick wave, and when my body calms, Lee pulls away with a mischevious smile, asking if I "wanna taste?"

"Yes, please."

He sticks his tongue in my mouth and we make out for a bit.

"Like it?"

"I do." I answer honestly.

"Me too." There's a slight pause as though there is more he wants to say but isn't sure how or what. "I want to have sex with you."

That's a way to do it. Don't get me wrong, I've been ready for this. There's no guessing what he means and what he wants. I just can't help but do that thing women do and question whether or not he'll still "like me in the morning."

Sex is something that didn't mean much to me until I experienced it differently. I don't wantsex with Lee to be something I feel obligated to do just because we've been dating for a while now and that's "what you do".

I want us to have sex because we both want to, because we care about each other and want to take the next step. I want to have sex with Lee because we're ready to make that level of commitment to one another. There are so many things about our connection that make me feel like Lee is the last first time sex partner I want to have.

I finally settle on "so, what are you gonna do about it?"

"Lay down."

Lee positions himself over me, missionary, and I reach between us and guide him in. He starts with a few short strokes, and then a full one. He's teasing me, and I'm trying to be patient, but I want him to fuck me. He picks up the pace and I squeeze my pelvic muscles, tightening around him. He slows again.

I groan in frustration, but say nothing. Lee gives me that charming grin and finally thrusts the length of his cock inside me. I am so ready and moans turn into "yes"es. He slows again.

"Fuck! Stop teasing me." My tone is playful but serious.

"Let's go to the bedroom. I don't really like having sex on the couch."

"Fine by me if you'll stop teasing so much."

Lee is not making any efforts to move to the bedroom. I laugh.

"Can't exactly go to the bedroom with you still inside me."

"I don't want to leave your pussy."

"I'll take that as a compliment." I clench my muscles around him.

"Okay, okay."

He pulls out and we make our way to the bedroom. I lean over the edge of the bed, Lee fucking me from behind. His motions now fast and hard as requested.

"Let's switch positions. I don't want to cum yet."

I flip onto my back, off the edge of the bed, and place one leg on each of Lee's shoulders. He moistens his fingers and plays with my clit while he fucks me. The air is filled with the sounds of our bodies and the intoxicating smell of our fluids.

"I won't last much longer. I want you to cum again. Do you have your vibrator?"

"Yeah, it's in my bag."

Lee runs for the hallway and returns with my entire bag. I locate my vibrator and we move into our final side laying position. There is no teasing to be had. He fucks me for the win and I place my vibrator directly on my clit. A few minutes later, Lee is ready and I'm not far behind him.

"I'm gonna cum."

"Fucking cum, baby."

And he does. His sound of his grunts, the feeling of his cock pulsing inside me, and the vibrations on my clit send me into my own orgasm.

Lee's cock retracts inside me and I tighten around him, teasing. It's too much and he extracts himself with a shudder. He rolls over on to his back and opens his arm, inviting me to cuddle. I rest on my stomach, in his arms, our legs intertwined.

"Do you still like me?" I ask half jokingly.

"I think my fondness for you is growing."

I thought, so is mine.

Accompanying Works

Too into you

Consider a moment,
What it might feel like
To be loved the way you love your child.
To get to be a part of every moment....
To be shelter from pain and lies.

What would it mean to have someone really there,
To be a beam of light in sickness and despair?

But what if the times weren't all that bad?
You could dine and laugh and sit.
Boundaries that were respected,
Dreams supported and encouraged.

Forgiveness,
Trust,
Vulnerability,
Truth.

If it's something you'd never had,
Or had with conditions,
Makes sense it would seem
One was too into you...

Seal the Deal

Scared would be an understatement.
Excited is not enough.
Enthralled might be getting there,
But love's too soon to touch.

I think of you on repeat.
So many smiles have crossed my face...
Intense, unnerving, titillating,
I woke up in a haze.

Started to dread the feelings that came.
Then I remembered the night before gaze.
As you moved yourself inside me,
Slowly and temperature rising...
So wet, so soft, gliding...
Wanting, craving, simply exhilarating.
Needing to feel you surrender,
To give myself to you completely,
But scared the next morning you'd think me needy.

So many reasons to not.
But so many more to go and grow and know you.
I feel myself. I feel you.
Not just inside me,
But all around me.
Held and caressed in your arms.
It's kinda pretty scary,
But look at this aware me...
This share me...

This true me...
So full of hope and sees the beauty,
To build this ship of relation.

The smiles and thrills are like drops on a coaster,
And I find myself simply wanting to be closer.
Let me in, let me know,
Please, just show
Me that part of you of us we can bring to exist,
That you see, and feel, it and want to persist.

I try to go slow down this path
But I'm failing.
And even though things have been
Less than smooth sailing, it's easy to want all of you.
The drinks and drugs I wonder about.
Could you? Would you?
What is that doubt that its not a thing?
I can't believe you mentioned a ring.
You got down on a knee for a simple request from me.
And I've got to admit it made my head spin,
In the best possible way, a bit.

I want you a part of my life.
It may be too early to say, but possibly be your wife.
Run my fingers through your hair,
And sit on your dick, and stare
Into your eyes, into your soul,
And kiss away and make it better
The hurt, the pain, the toll.

To pour my love into the cracks.
Soothe the bruises and remove any knick knacks
And garbage of anything unkind.
Love you like no other
In body, soul and mind.
How my heart can learn to trust you...

Even when it was feeling hurt, betrayed and lied to.

Delight me, tease me, kiss me, squeeze me,
Fuck me, make love to me, I want you to cum in me.
Be mine, I'm yours. Let's explore each other.
Tell me the truth, the words of how you feel.
I can sense it and it feels like something real.
Just say it and seal the deal.

Lee

Opened my head, my legs, my bed...
What do you expect?
You get what you want. You leave me with none...
It's just like the rest.

It's partly rejection, and partly redemption
and vulnerability and fuck... we're moving so fast.
Or is it just me? Have I lost my fucking mind?
Are these highs so high and lows so low?
You've opened me up and it's like I don't fucking know.

You get my hopes up.
Well, I let you anyway.
No condom, just trust.
Feels like I maybe made a mistake.
Blinded by my own desires, and a man who says things he thinks
I'd want to hear...
Am I that idiot who does dumb shit for "love"?

Fuck I need sleep.

Bullseye

I knew I was falling last Wednesday when you came over and we were sitting on my couch and you had your feet up and you just leaned and rested and relaxed and told me about your day as I ran my fingers through your hair.

I knew I was a gonner on Thursday when we were lying in your bed snuggling and talking and I was rubbing your chest and I said, I think this is my favorite part.

When I wanted to tell people about you and slowly did tell a few, I knew it was real for me and I wasn't gonna be able to keep it to myself much longer.

When I told my cousin that I loved you I thought, oh boy, I'm in this for real.

I want to say it to you, but I don't want you to feel cornered or like you need to fight/flight. I want you to tell me because you love me and you want me to know.

My truth

The truth is I love you.
But I want you to know...
If you don't feel the same...
Please don't say so.

There's really no rush...
For me it's simply a choice.
But the challenge really is
To give those words a voice.

I'm not scared you don't love me.
And maybe that's a bit presumptive.
But your words, actions, and touch
Fill my mind, heart and body in a way that's consumptive.

So what if I say it
And you don't say it back?
Or maybe, even worse, you don't mean it...
And it feels like a slap?

But the truth is the truth;
It will always come to light.
I love you, Lee.
And saying it just feels right.

Pep Talk

Afraid to want
What I have no guarantee I can have...
What a horrible depressing thought.
It really makes me sad.

To watch a love run away,
Slipping through my fingers everyday,
Knowing I can't make him stay,
So all I guess I can do is weigh
my options.

But that sounds small and stupid to me.
How a bored buy curious cat might climb a tree.
Yet the view from up there might be pretty clear;
The view up there much wider than here.

Get some perspective.
Remember who you are.
You bring so much to the table.
Even with your many scars.

Don't let it stop you from loving.
Keep dreaming and hoping and being.
What's for you will come.
Awe yourself and find some meaning
In the big and little... any win.
Support your self, always, and again.

You have so much to offer, and so much to share.
Don't let a man who's not ready
keep you in his limited sphere.

I love you, I love you, I love you.
I can hear my little self say.
One day love will happen.
And it will overwhelm you in every way...
Greater than you've ever imagined,
Shinier than a polished piece of glass...
You fucking shine girl, and he can kiss your ass.

Using

It's too painful right now
To think about moving on.
Knowing how long I waited for something this strong.
I'd convinced myself you were it,
        that you were in fact the one.
That your working on yourself was a bonus,
        albeit not always fun.
Yet I thought we could weather any storm...
And you felt I was too into you,
        that my feelings were too strong.

I don't know how to love, in any conditional way.
Did you ever stop to consider having that might make you shy away?
Instead you bundled inward and kept yourself from knowing...
Pulling and tugging the opposite direction, to stop our relationship from growing.

What hurts the most is somewhere in there I let myself
        believe ...
You were my last chance, and now was time to grieve.
To greive the loss of hope I had
In getting what I wanted...
To be with someone body and mind.
To cherish, have and hold them – dashed.

Where do I go from here? How do I fid myself again?
Sex? That's it? That's all you want? We can't even be friends?
So I settle for body, no mind; holding not having...

Trying to convince myself it's okay
On the mind it's quite taxing.

It's fine for right now, but someday it won't be.
I'll find that strong, that brave, unsettling new me.
Who knows who I'll end up with. Maybe it'll be a new you.
But I'm not holding my breath.
I'm just using you to fuck too.

Shower musings

I gave and gave and gave.
You took and took and took.
You gave and gave and gave.
I mistook, mistook, mistook.

Attaching and assigning
Meaning to your words.
Believing all your actions,
Some crazy things I heard...
Or rather, made up and told myself lies.
Made it quite difficult to say those goodbyes.

I'm glad to have you back in any way.
I guess I know it's not enough.
Kind of feels like a mess.
But my heart isn't in shambles, and
I'm learning and growing too...
So, for now it's okay
In those private moments just me and you.

You're not mine

You never really were, were you?
Just a matter of time.
I'll always be grateful but sometimes it hurts.
In my heart of hearts I yearn for you,
Believing this could work.

So, instead, I take another path.
Accepting what I can get...
Knowing I'm amazing, but waiting around for your dick.

I know it's fucking stupid, and I'm probably lying to myself;
But I'll do this as long as I can because I don't have anything else.

That's not in a sad way or depressive style of emotion,
It's simply that no one else right now is requesting or needing my devotion.

But I guess that's not true either.
I am the one who needs me.
I am the one who needs to learn to quiet the noise and be.

One day I'll get there, or something will change;
But for now I'll stay in this zone of whatever the fuck this is.

I look forward to looking back and laughing from a warm and loving place.
How I prayed for you, beloved, that you would find your way to this space
Remembering who you are and what you bring to the table.
You are strong and so loved. You were blinded by the fable you told yourself.

It's lovely to have you back. Those many nights of tears and sadness I'm sure were hard in fact.
I can't tell you what happens or where the journey takes you, but you have what it takes and I promise you it's worth it.

Be gentle with you and offer her some grace.
It can be tough in this physical and limited place.
Get to know yourself and find the truth inside.
Your mind is boundless and ready for a hell of a ride filled with love...
And yes some loss, but it's nothing you can't handle.

Feel feel feel, be open
Meditate and be honest with others and yourself
The thought will happen but don't believe them all
Put it up to question and see where you land.
If it doesn't sit right in your spirit, let it go from your hand, your mind, whatever is holding it.

Do the dishes and do them with flare.
When magic happens show gratitude.
Live in love.
Still in quiet.
Peace in empty.

You don't get it do you

I love you unconditionally.
I want to help lift you when you're feeling down,
Hold you when you need comfort,
Fuck your when you need release,
Joke with you when you need a laugh,
Sit with you when you need a cry,
Remind you just how handsome I think you are, every day that goes by.

I want to be your friend.
I want to be your lover.
I want to be the person you open up to, not run away from for cover.

Let's grown and learn together,
Encourage each others art.
Speak to me in ways unheard,
The language of your heart.

Share your life with me.
Just as I will also.

The last time they were here

You were on the other side of most of my texts.
You had lied, and so were trying to make your way back in.
As I waited at the stage door, not talking to you this time,
Remembering how I couldn't wait to get to you to kiss you and make us, yours and mine.
This time was a bit tormentful, honestly a bit of a drag.
I know of course I'll see you soon, but only to be had in body.

I love you Lee. I fucking love you, unconditionally and always will.
How do I win this battle of mine between my heart and the space between my ears?
How does it work outside of together,
But so well still in your arms?
How do I react when you ask if I'm coming in...
Inviting me to that space next to you, and across your chest,
Where you tell me your life and secret things that keep you from getting rest?
You say if this ends, that you'd be fine.
Of course that's the case, but why does it feel like you should be mine?

I'd move mountains to make your dreams come true.
And when we're apart I long to be with you,
not as a sitting duck but a partner in life, sharing and being present in time.
Why does this work in only one way?
Do you really not feel things that make you want to stay?
Are you denying yourself for the sake of some lie you told yourself, like you hurt her once so don't try?

I never asked for commitment, just to spend the night
Not for the sake of intimacy, just hot fucks over over and over to daylight.
Instead I got a speech on what I associated with my worth,
That you simply didn't love me, and wasn't sure who you were becoming.
You couldn't give me what you thought I wanted and deserved.
You made a choice and shut me out,
Not giving me the chance to evaluate and decide
How I wanted to be at the dance.

So I offered up the one thing I thought you couldn't say no to, my body.
But I was wrong and for months I put in work to make myself better to be strong again, trying to forget the strong connection I had to you, the one I wanted to be my man.

Then one day I ran into you and it seemed you tried to hide.
I wasn't gonna call you out, but I knew that I was wrong too and myself tried to deny.
Hide that my heart beat faster, and a smile plagued my face,
Hide that all I wanted was to be in your embrace,
To hold you close to me and smell you so near.

And what do you know you responded.
And seemingly out of nowhere,
You brought up you were thinking of my offer of body, with no strings there.
Honestly I was horny and figured I'd take what I could get.
I simply don't have the time or desire to find a new partner yet.
In fact it makes me weary to think I need to try again.
Though need is strong I suppose, I am an independent woman.

My therapist says it's okay if I'm not ready yet, but she thinks I'm compromising and doesn't understand why I think I can't get
All that I want in a relationship, a real one where I'm loved back.
I guess if I really admit it I've never really believed it would happen

for me.

So it's hard to let go of a man who made me feel it was happening, 35 years in and finally the real deal.
The beginning was easy to be distant, so many questions and uncertainties.
Then I got comfortable and let myself believe that perhaps this was real, something I could achieve.
It's more than just him and who he was, it was the feeling that I didn't doubt that we were in love.
I wasn't scared of what he wouldn't say because he showed me. I wasn't afraid of what he did say because I knew at any point either of us could walk away. Though I must admit, I had every intention to stay.

Perhaps he did me a favor.
I've certainly grown quite a lot.
I refuse now to allow myself to simply sit and rot and mourn someone who doesn't love me in that way I want, but how do I know he doesn't, even though it's not the same as before?

Enjoy whatever this is, till your heart and mind align.
Be open to possibilities should another man stand in line.
Try not to lose yourself while you've got one foot out the door.
Lee continues living life with no real regard for what you've given freely and don't quite value yourself, why should he?

One day, one day, one day, something will click.
I'm excited for that day for you beloved.
Expect the constant, change.

With you

Of course I want to see you,
But not in the way you think.
I want to see you next to me brushing our teeth at the sink.
I want to see your hand in mine as we walk down the city street.
I want to see your smile across the table as we grab a bite to eat.
I want to see you in front of a crowd enthralling us with your words.
I want to see your feet kicked up on the couch having coffee in the morning listening to the birds.
I want to see you enter me and feel our bodies in motion.
I want to see you get what you've worked so hard for, earning that promotion.
I want to see your ups and downs, your easy and your hard.
I want to see you as you and get to be a part.

You don't have to let me.
The choice is yours to make.
I certainly won't put a hold on my life.
That would be a mistake.

But I wish you all the best,
And the joy and all the love.
I'm so grateful for the time we had,
And the orgasm inducing fucks.

Boy from Indiana

I fell in love with a boy from Indiana.
Well, he was a grown ass man.
He was charming and sexy and the most interesting one
I'd come to know.
We always had good chats,
And fun whereever we went.
The sex was amazing.
The relationship, time well spent.
I don't know what happened,
Or where things fell apart.
He said I seemed too interested in him.
But I just loved him how I was taught.
It's okay he didn't love me back.
I've learned and grown so much.
The part that sucks is the lies he told.
Maybe a new start as friends, an empty thought turned cold.
I made him tell me he didn't love me
Or want to be with me,
Regardless of if it was true.
I needed the audio visual.
He broke up with me over voice note, albeit a very long one,
But the two days before my birthday part also sucked as well.
I offered my body, which he declined.
But a few months later he changed his mind.
It lasted just under a month, which was no surprise to me,
I just felt a little hurt cause even just sex wasn't something I was "worth".
It's all my world, coming from my mind, but I'd love to hear his

truth.
Not as an excuse for treating me shitty or even an explanation.
Just the truth, just because.
Was I a bad girlfriend? Did I talk too much? When did the realization hit him that he was done?
We see each other somewhat often, because we're not far apart.
It's cordial when we happen to meet but it bums me out we can't actually be friends.
He talks a lot and says things he thinks others want to hear.
All I ever asked him for, but once, was the truth.
So why does he consume my brain waves? My "Roman empire" as the kids might say.
Lack of understanding. I left any obligations in the year before, then firmly closed the door. Might not have locked it though or thrown away the key.
I know he'll never knock or even come close
So what the hell am I doing?
Let that boy from Indiana go.

Missing cock

I'd hoped you'd eat me on the roof,
Or tied me to my bed.
I'd hoped I'd squirt on your cock,
And then you'd eat my pussy well.
I'd hoped you'd fuck my mouth,
With my head off the side of the bed.
I'd hoped you'd smack my ass, and
Fuck me hard till I begged you to slow instead.

I'd hoped we'd fuck in a hotel room,
Or your kitchen island,
Or in the shower,
Possibly even one day in a car.
I'd considered letting you fuck me in the ass,
Even sticking my finger in yours.

I'd hoped you'd suck my nipples, once the piercings healed.
I'd hoped I'd watch you masturbate to me playing with myself.
I'd hoped you'd fill me with your cum multiple times in the night.
I'd hoped I'd wake up to your tongue on my clit, sun shining bright.

I'd hoped we'd fuck the rest of our lives,
Checking fantasies off our lists.
Maybe it was never really you,
Seems like it's your cock I miss.

No lies, some hurt, all truth

I know these are usually short and sweet,
but I'm so fucking tired of being nice and neat.
So here's your fucking thank you,
and, though this may sound crass,
take your silly smirk and shove it up your ass.

It's true that I still love you,
but I fucking love me more.
I remind myself everyday of that before my feet hit the floor.
I'm stopping this rejection cycle—
Third time is not the charm.

Probably seems like I'm coming in hot.
Just dedicating honestly and with a lot of thought.
I acknowledge the part I played and what I allowed.
It's a journey, but I've forgiven myself and
lifted the heartbreak cloud.

No obligation, no expectation, nothing is required from you.
Read it, don't read it, you'll do what you want to do.
So let's revisit words that eventually turned into the messy rest:
My love, I wish you the best.

Afterword

If you made it to this and read it, cool. Thanks. It's been a little while now and "I" would like you to know, she's well. She still thinks about Lee and will always love him and want the best for him, but she's loving on herself right now. Its a life long process.

Pete did respond and they're on good terms.

Also, please remember, just in case you forgot, that "I" and Pete and Lee and Denise are all not real. This is a work of fiction.

Yes, really.

Acknowledgements

Thank you Jackie, Lauren and Lillian for your support over the years in all of my artistic endeavors. I know that some of them were not your favorite and probably tough to sit through; but having you there meant more than you know.

To Brigette, Curtis, Dana, Shaun, Trena and Dr. K...I can't begin to thank you for all the time you spent listening to me blabber. Thank you for loving on me, offering advice and empathizing.

M, thank you for the idea that I could do this.

Daddio, I'm so, so, so incredibly grateful for the way our relationship has grown. Thank you for being willing to hop on a plane, pick up the phone and hear things. Thank you for encouraging me to "turn the fork".

www.ingramcontent.com/pod-product-compliance
Lightning Source LLC
LaVergne TN
LVHW090536110826
845146LV00003B/1126

* 9 7 9 8 2 1 8 6 5 2 7 1 5 *